STARSHIPS, SPEEDERS & SPACE STATIONS

Adapted by Christopher Nicolas
Illustrated by Alan Batson, Heather Martinez, Chris Kennett, Pilot Studio, Patrick Spaziante, Caleb Meurer, and Micky Rose

 A GOLDEN BOOK • NEW YORK

© & ™ 2017 LUCASFILM LTD. All rights reserved. Published in the United States by Golden Books, an imprint of Random House Children's Books, a division of Penguin Random House LLC, 1745 Broadway, New York, NY 10019, and in Canada by Penguin Random House Canada Limited, Toronto. Originally published in slightly different form in 2017 by Golden Books. Golden Books, A Golden Book, A Little Golden Book, the G colophon, and the distinctive gold spine are registered trademarks of Penguin Random House LLC.

rhcbooks.com

ISBN 978-1-9848-4833-8 (trade)—ISBN 978-1-9848-4834-5 (ebook)

Printed in the United States of America

10 9 8 7 6 5 4 3 2 1

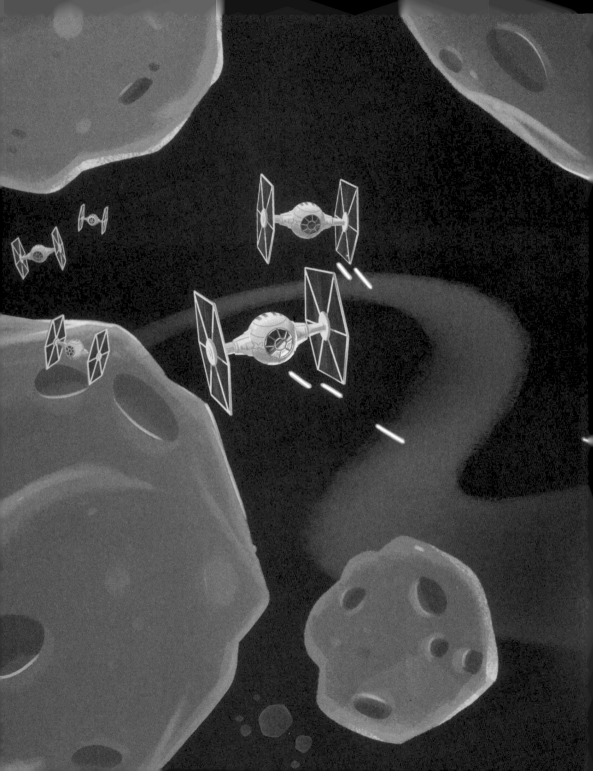

A long time ago in a galaxy far, far away . . .

Amazing machines sped across the land, soared through the skies, and rocketed through space.

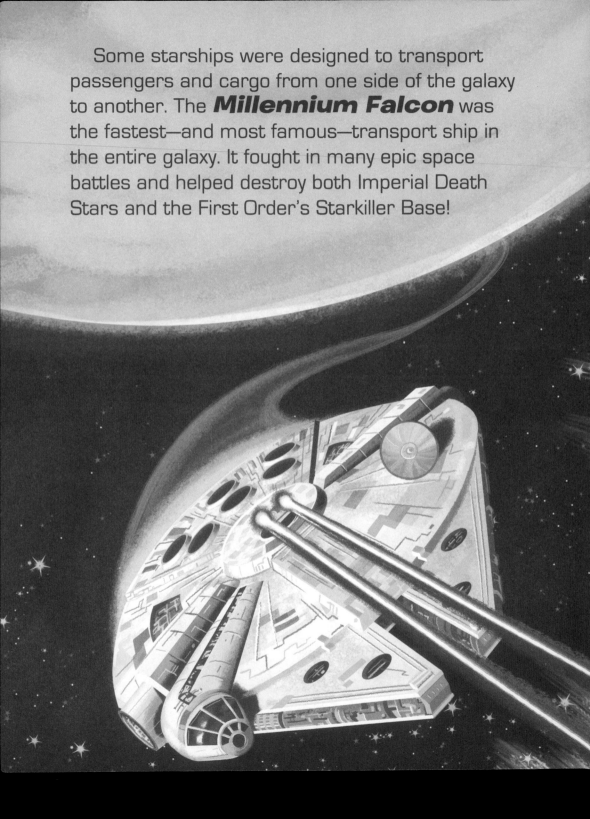

Some starships were designed to transport passengers and cargo from one side of the galaxy to another. The **Millennium Falcon** was the fastest—and most famous—transport ship in the entire galaxy. It fought in many epic space battles and helped destroy both Imperial Death Stars and the First Order's Starkiller Base!

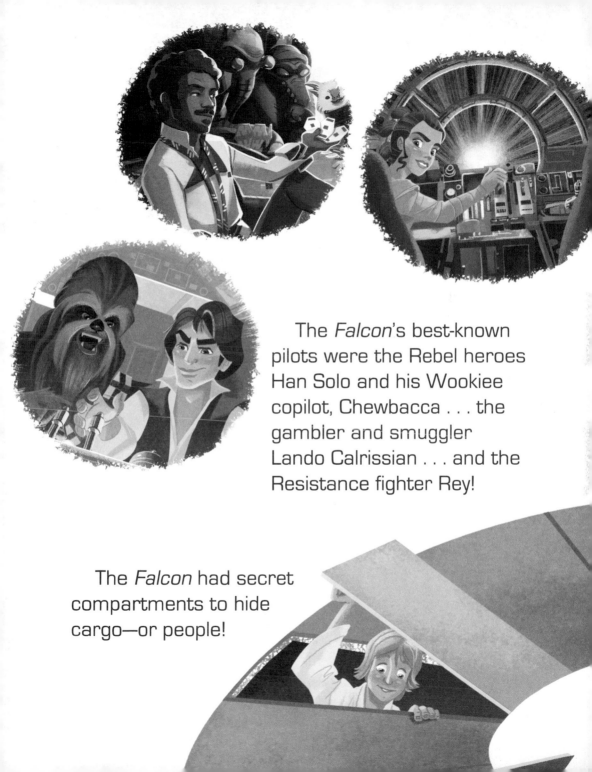

The *Falcon*'s best-known pilots were the Rebel heroes Han Solo and his Wookiee copilot, Chewbacca . . . the gambler and smuggler Lando Calrissian . . . and the Resistance fighter Rey!

The *Falcon* had secret compartments to hide cargo—or people!

Battleships were built for battle! Gigantic Imperial Star Destroyers and Super Star Destroyers cast a shadow of fear over Rebels and Resistance fighters throughout the galaxy.

Star Destroyers were so enormous, other starships were carried inside them!

Starfighters were small, fast, and nimble ships that were able to dart through swarming space battles for quick attacks on their enemies.

Brave Rebel pilots flew these fighters in the epic battle that ended with the defeat of the Galactic Empire once and for all!

The **X-wing** fighter was shaped like an X when its wings were extended for battle. With his trusty droid copilot BB-8, Poe Dameron flew his X-wing on special missions for the Resistance!

TIE fighters were piloted by the Galactic Empire and the First Order.

They could be easily recognized by their hexagonal wings and the screaming roar of their engines.

Darth Vader piloted a special customized TIE fighter and destroyed many Rebel starfighters.

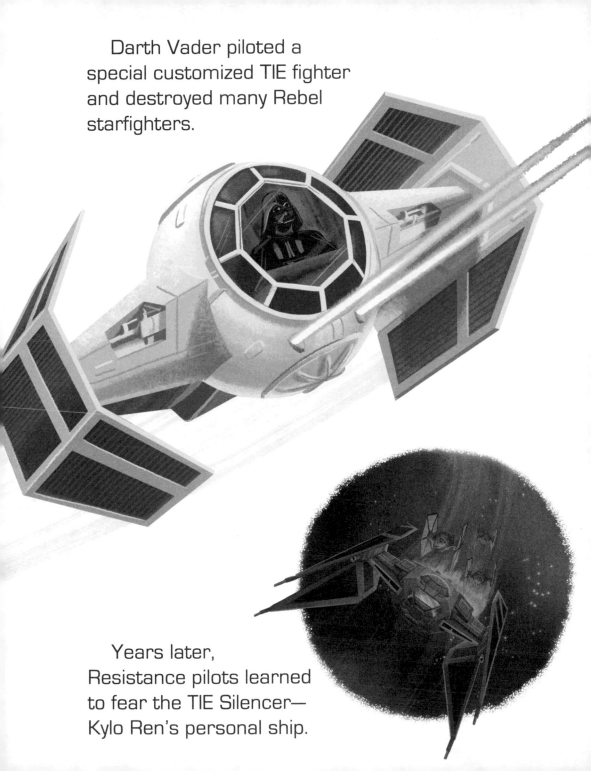

Years later, Resistance pilots learned to fear the TIE Silencer— Kylo Ren's personal ship.

Space stations were enormous mobile bases that could travel through star systems. Some were as big as moons!

Death Stars were the ultimate weapons of the Galactic Empire. Entire planets could be vaporized by their powerful superlasers! And their tractor beams could drag unsuspecting ships inside for capture.

The First Order's
Starkiller Base was
even bigger and more
destructive than the two Death
Stars combined!

Supreme Leader Snoke and
Kylo Ren hoped that it would
eliminate the Republic and the
Resistance once and for all.

Speeders were
designed for . . . speed!
Landspeeders
sped across the land . . .

snow speeders
soared over snowy terrain . . .

airspeeders flew
through busy city skyways . . .

. . . and **Gungan subs** traveled underwater! Jar Jar Binks guided Qui-Gon Jinn and Obi-Wan Kenobi through Naboo's core to rescue Queen Amidala.

Speeder bikes

could carry only one
passenger. But they were
fast and very nimble,
making them perfect for . . .

fast escapes . . .

sneak attacks . . .

. . . or scouting!
   When an Imperial Scout Trooper discovered the Rebels on planet Endor, Princess Leia had to stop him—before the secret mission to disable the Death Star's shields was revealed!

Walkers were able to traverse rough terrains by walking on mechanical legs! And their hulking animal-like shapes struck fear into those who opposed them.

The First Order dispatched huge imperial AT-M6 walkers to attack the secret Resistance base on the planet Crait.

A **conveyex** traveled along rails like a train. These heavily armored vehicles were used to transport the Empire's most valuable cargo.

Young Han Solo and Chewbacca once made a daring attempt to steal precious fuel from a conveyex—while it was traveling at top speed!

Some ships were droids! The Trade Federation's pilotless **Vulture Droids** and **Trifighters** made quick work of Republic starfighters during the clone wars.

Some ships were feared! The ruthless bounty hunter Jango Fett—and later his son Boba Fett—piloted *Slave I* throughout the galaxy, capturing wanted humans and aliens for a reward.

Some ships were royal! The shimmering silver **Naboo Royal Starship** flew the Queen across the galaxy on missions of goodwill.

Starships, **speeders**, and
space stations played crucial roles in
the epic struggle between good and evil.
Where would the galaxy be without them . . . ?